Curious Fables

M.V. Montgomery

Winter Goose
PUBLISHING
where words take flight

Winter Goose Publishing
45 Lafayette Road #114
North Hampton, NH 03862

www.wintergoosepublishing.com
Contact Information: info@wintergoosepublishing.com

Curious Fables

COPYRIGHT © 2017 by M.V. Montgomery

First Edition, June 2017

Cover Design by Winter Goose Publishing
Typeset by Odyssey Publishing

ISBN: 978-1-941058-68-8

Published in the United States of America

To Jessica Kristie and James Koukis

Contents

The Werewolf Who Found Inner Peace

A certain man spent most of his life indoors, moving between condo, car, and his office, which was located high in a highrise building in the middle of a busy city.

At a business lunch one day, he ordered a dish containing raw meat. It had been killed just the night before, the waiter said. Maybe that's the reason it was so expensive.

The waiter brought out a dish of animal parts with dipping sauces. The man picked up a leg and took a bite—but too late, saw that it already had teeth marks in it, and drool.

The next night the man was at home when the full moon appeared. He started to feel odd. He wasn't one for exercise, had let his LA Fitness membership lapse. But for some reason this night he opened his window, not worrying about the loss of AC.

He breathed fresh air, and it was good. Then the idea of going for a moonlit jaunt in the park seized him and he clambered down the fire escape.

In anticipation, he started running, then dropped to his hands and knees and loped. He had a dim consciousness of his skin turning prickly, of his sense of smell growing razor-sharp.

He paused to sniff at a flock of pigeons. They looked so plump and smooth, he couldn't help wondering what it would be like to bite into one. And tonight his whole mood was, *Why not?*

He grabbed the plumpest and juiciest bird he could find, twisted its neck, and took a bite so deep the juices popped in his mouth.

The next day he awoke with feathers in his teeth. When he checked his pillow for holes, it looked fine; it just had rather a lot of shaggy hair on it. The man assumed he was balding and made a mental note to send away for one of those cures.

Otherwise, he felt great. He'd had plenty of healthy exercise the night before (though he couldn't have remembered this). And since he was the Big Boss and could go in to work when he wanted, why not take the morning off?

The man began leading a more balanced existence, rejuvenated by his reconnection with nature. He ate a healthier diet, cutting out meats and replacing them with vegetables, fruits, and whole grains. More and more he found himself governed not by his work schedule, but by natural cycles. And while he'd previously been thought a sexist who did not believe women up to brutal corporate tasks, he now found himself promoting them actively to make up for past wrongs, and listening to all workers with renewed interest. His reputation among employees soared, because here was a man of empathy!

To fraternize with others outside the workplace seemed a presumption of familiarity, however, so the man spent his evenings per usual, reading. He kept his TV turned off except for PBS, finding the medium too violent for his tastes. If there was one thing he couldn't stomach, it was scenes of people hurting each other.

He invariably woke up during full moon cycles to feathers and confusion. Only in time did he put two-and-two together, after checking his security video. He watched intently as a shaggy beast crawled into his apartment through the window and wondered, *Could that really be me?* The next night, when he started to feel funny like that, he snapped a selfie.

Yes, perhaps it was him on the *outside*—but it wasn't who

he felt himself to be *inside*. In fact, it was everything he didn't like: the hairiness, coarse behavior, jacked-up muscles, and weaponized teeth. Such features might be thought "masculine," but he had rejected brutality in any form.

And so the man scheduled a gender reversal operation. He'd never seen a movie about a female werewolf—maybe a little cheat would do the trick?

In preparation for the operation, the man began a hormone regimen to soften his features and help him to resist his urges. He ordered bars for his windows and restraints too complicated for a clumsy-fingered wolfman to figure out. Such measures ought to keep him contained until dawn and reason returned.

The next full moon, the restraints held. He'd made a point of eating a huge dinner, a whole tofurkey, and the beast inside was so slugged out on the cheat-meat that it didn't protest much. It did bother the man, however, that his mind continued to steer so out of control.

He enrolled in a transcendental meditation class. And practiced as often as work allowed—until he stopped going to the office altogether. The man had enough money already, and the more he meditated, the less he cared about it.

He shaved his head and fasted, and the transformation in his appearance was quite startling, to the point that he thought he could skip the operation and just live with the man in the mirror.

Next the man sold his condo and bought a place on the beach where he could welcome the sun.

Over time, his skills sharpened. Because he'd conditioned himself to resist intense monthly urges, he had great reserves of spiritual energy. He found he no longer needed the restraints.

He began to welcome the monthly appearance of the Wolf, to regard it as a spirit-animal sent to him as a gift.

Years passed, and the man wondered, had there really ever been a Wolf, or was this only a name he'd given to what others call ego?

Mentally, he was now one with the Wolf. He was one with No-Wolf too.

One night as he sat cross-legged on the shore, an enormous full moon broke over the waves and he felt his sense of being dissolve, melt into his surroundings.

He howled a triumphant final howl and let the beast go.

The Witch Who Took a Look at Herself

Once a woman was married to a decent sort of man who, for the most part, loved and took care of her. She thought she could make herself "happy" by following the usual protocol of marriage, house, and child, but it can be a dangerous thing to put quotes around that word and turn happiness into a concept.

The couple had a beautiful daughter whom everyone thought the image of her mother. The woman was uncomfortable with this category of praise because she'd always celebrated her own energy and youth. The relegation to an older generation felt like a demotion, and her relationship to her own child took on the air of competition.

It didn't help matters much that her husband seemed to want to spend all his time adoring the little girl, which meant less time for her.

The woman soon regarded her married life from a whole different aspect. Perhaps her husband had neglected her and her needs all along? Perhaps her marriage had never been truly happy, after all? It wasn't just her saying this. It was all her Internet friends too.

She started to seek attention elsewhere, pursuing Ashley Madison kinds of affairs. Another protocol followed: separation, divorce, an ironclad custody schedule.

In time, she friended an online gentleman who was sympathetic when she told him she'd married a jerk. He was also a decade older, offering the welcome prospect of rendering her comparatively youthful. He called the woman his angel and baby doll though she was fast approaching forty.

Mother and daughter, at this point in time, made an odd pair. One dressed twenty years younger; the other had become so used to caring for herself she'd attained the wise air of someone much older.

The woman encouraged strangers to mistake them for sisters and occasionally pulled off this flattering ruse. But a hard look in the mirror eventually revealed the beginnings of eyelid sag and chin droop, and hair which had lost its natural sheen. Normal enough to you and me, who understand that youth is a junk bond that never pays out, but a tragedy to someone whose whole raison d'être was to reverse-age.

The woman became a health fanatic, exercising to the point she wore out machines, and taking nutritional supplements by the Chinese shipping container-full. She dumped her second husband when others had the effrontery to associate her with him, age-wise. Her daughter became a successful scientist and married, but the woman could not smile for any of the wedding pictures. She'd begun frequenting plastic surgeons and too much scar tissue had built up around the tight mask of her face.

Then her daughter did something hurtful, unspeakable, shameful, for which the woman never forgave her—she became pregnant.

She scolded the young woman over the phone, even encouraged her to have an abortion to preserve her "professional career." Becoming a grandparent was the kind of life crisis the woman most feared. Fortunately for the girl, her mother's surgically plumped lips couldn't accommodate her rant and her words weren't intelligible.

The woman put down the receiver and wanted to cry, but her tear ducts were sealed. Yet her emotions had reached the point of overflow and needed release. She threw back her head and yelled a yell of existential rage. There was a ripping sound as her cheeks parted, exposing her gums. One eye popped out like a ping-pong ball, and her chin sagged to where her wishbone would be, if human beings had been granted a wishbone.

You'd think the woman's next move would've been to dial 911, but it was inconceivable to her that the EMTs might see her like this. So instead, she picked up her eyeball like a contact lens and popped it back into its socket, where it remained, slightly askew. Then she smashed her mirror and vowed never to look in one again.

I dislike the word "witch" and apologize in advance for any sexist connotations. But that is the very word children around town began using to taunt her. When the taunting became unbearable, the woman moved to the country. The abandoned farmhouse she occupied there inevitably became known as "the witch's house."

For years she remained in isolation, imagining herself a princess in exile. She lived on nuts and berries and road-kill, making herself vomit afterwards to maintain a svelte figure. And washed her clothes in a nearby stream, which is where this tale ends.

One day while scrubbing a blouse on which the designer label was now scarcely legible, the woman leaned too far and caught a reflection in the water.

At first, the distorted image didn't even register to her as her own.

Then suddenly she began to shake with laughter. She laughed from inner reserves she didn't know she had, laughed as she hadn't in years.

In a moment, she perceived that she'd lived in a world of illusion.

The old woman's remaining days would pass as before—with one notable exception. Each morning as she drew water from the stream, she always took an extra long look at her reflection. And laughed again.

They found her at that very spot—face down in the water, a beatific expression on her face. Country living had certainly agreed with her: she looked more like somebody's kindly grandmother than a witch. Her face had grown tan and wizened, and most of the deep wrinkles on it were smile lines.

The superstitious people in town came to believe that the stream had restorative powers, and still drop by to fill their plastic jugs on weekends.

But if you ask me, true magic power derives from not taking oneself too seriously, from realizing that this whole culture of youth and glamour we've created is essentially worthless.

The Hideous, Many-Tentacled Relationship

She and He had carried on for many years after college as just friends. Then one day, when they were at their favorite diner bemoaning the lack of opportunities on the dating scene, an invisible presence took shape in the air and hovered between them.

We should go out, He suddenly said, out of nowhere.

Is that a pitch? She giggled.

They sat there and anatomized their recent e-mails and emoticons, coming to the surprise conclusion that perhaps there was something there, after all. It was a joyous moment of discovery.

The next night, had one observed She and He on their first "date," a few basic differences would have emerged: (1) they weren't at their usual place, but in a restaurant with a scenic ocean overlook; (2) they admired this romantic view excessively; and (3) they fumbled through much of the rest of the dinner conversation also.

He provided her with a chatty weather report. She translated the menu for him. *Awk*-ward.

It had become a table for three: She, He, and the Relationship.

What eventually got the juices flowing may have been the proximity to the oceanfront. In going down a checklist of potential couples activities, She came up with the not-so-novel idea of going on a cruise.

The proposal caught him unawares. Reflexively, He pulled out his phone and commenced Googling. Really, they both shone in situations like this, when it came to choosing vacation destinations or working out finances.

Preparatory to voyaging out, what a lot of collaborative decisions to make! There were passports to update, shots to get. There were clothes-shopping trips. Once when She came out of a dressing room to ask his opinion of a swimsuit, He felt the stirrings of *something* like desire. He executed an awkward hug. She pulled him back into the changing area, closed the curtain, and kissed him.

Now they had a story to tell.

At some imprecise point, they began referring to the upcoming cruise as a "honeymoon." With that boundary firmly established, each enjoyed playfully tantalizing the other to see how far things might go.

By this point they were speaking of the Relationship in the third person: Do you think we should tell others about the Relationship? Won't they be surprised?

They nurtured the Relationship, helped it grow.

The day of the cruise finally arrived. They joined other couples on deck to wave to perfect strangers on shore. Then tromped rather solemnly to their cabin, which was a sanitary cubicle just like all others.

But . . .

It had all been a big mistake. They simply couldn't overcome their awkwardness, didn't feel like doting upon each other in that way. Indeed, they couldn't wait to get out of that room so they could breathe free.

Let the Relationship slither off to die in some dark corner. Good riddance!

They attended several shipboard performances that evening, but it seemed like the point was to pretend to be entertained by precisely the sort of singers and entertainers they'd always mocked in college. Or to become an essentially mindless alimentary canal affixed to some buffet table.

He grew seasick and couldn't eat, anyway. Wasn't this one of those supposedly fun things we swore we'd never do? he moaned.

Who are you, David Foster Wallace? She teased.

The good-natured ribbing was back. *They* were back.

But what of the Relationship? Wouldn't it still be lurking there in the room, waiting expectantly, hoping for a relapse?

It was too late to jump ship, but they were informed that two single cabins could be arranged, if they wouldn't mind waiting another day.

In the meantime, She and He decided to set off on an island expedition. Why not?

They felt good, rambunctious enough to ditch the herd and find a private spot on the Splenda-like sand, where they could make cracks about the rest of the tour group to their hearts' content.

They did not look back to the ship, nor notice that from it a sort of black blob had begun swimming toward them. It bobbed ominously on the waves.

It made landfall behind them, sneaking up just as they'd started to forget themselves again: Had they abandoned the romance prematurely? Now that they'd found their own corner of paradise, wasn't it time to play Adam and Eve?

She began looking at him with loosened-bridled lust—then drew back.

He leaned over to kiss her—then thought, *No, this isn't right.*

Too late! A long tentacle encircled her neck. The force of a hundred suction cups drew him down onto her body. The Relationship had returned with a vengeance. It did not want to die.

She and He gazed at each other. Silently, they understood that if they were going to kill this hydra, it was going to take a herculean effort. So they each grabbed a tentacle and began pulling.

Snap! Off one came.

Snap! There went another.

But the Relationship would not be so easily quelled. It slapped the man silly with half-a-dozen flailing arms. It sank its hideous beak into the woman's flank, causing her to scream out in pain.

Fortunately He was able to grab a nearby rock and send it crunching down on the pallial cavity. She found a shard of driftwood and plunged it repeatedly into the monster's spongy side. They didn't stop until they were both covered in inky blood and the Relationship lay in tatters beside them. Digging a deep hole in the sand, they decided to bury it right there, for keeps.

And then, panting and exhausted, they just took a break and relaxed side-by-side on the beach.

The cruise ship blared its warning: time to leave.

She and He dared to linger on that dreadful shore only a moment longer—fingers and toes almost touching, but not quite.

Jonathan's Smart Suit

Once a boy arrived very late in the lives of two people who made just about the most unlikely parents you could ever imagine.

His father was an engineer who specialized in robots and AI, with the electric socket-hair of a true mad scientist. He had never been close to a woman. Jonathan's genetic mother was a celebrated B-movie actress from the 1970s who'd been declared dead a decade prior. The scientist, an obsessive fan of her sci-fi work, had ordered one of her cryogenically frozen ova off Craigslist. He kept it in a freezer until the mood was right.

Conception was achieved one dark, sweaty night in the lab. The incubation of the little homunculus in a host mother followed.

It turned out that this folksy, no-nonsense woman grew quite attached to the child in utero, and subsequently managed to insinuate herself into the mad scientist's favor as a housekeeper-nanny. Her name was Imelda.

Thus Jonathan was born into quite a strange household.

The baby was a late crawler until his father invented a harness to raise him from the floor and propel him along. A late walker, until his father invented for him a pair of stilts to fit inside his suit of clothes and send him sprinting ahead of other boys.

Toilet training was skipped altogether, because Jonathan's

father invented a device for suctioning waste and compacting it into a disposable nappy. No Freudian trauma necessary.

Disturbingly, the boy was also late to talk. Beginning to suspect he may have purchased a rotten egg, yet wishing to make the best of it, Jonathan's father invented a special head harness with speech software and enhanced vocabulary and translation capabilities. These allowed the boy to wholly bypass the baby babble phase. Soon the verbally slow child was intoning like Orson Welles.

So that the lad should not go about bumping his head, a siren affixed to the top of the helmet emitted a warning signal. Sensors on the suit's skin also fed information to a receptor in the headpiece and all but eliminated the usual childhood collection of cuts, splinters, and scars.

But to be injury-free was not a sufficiently lofty aspiration for the son of a bona fide genius. No, he must be the smartest in his class! Thus to Jonathan's special suit were added many enhancements: ambient data detectors, adaptive programming, and memory apps which allowed him to draw upon a rich store of experiences—personal, tribal, even archetypal.

The suit was moreover health-regulating, pushing the boy to reach his maximum potential. For example, if young Jonathan might be disposed to do a perfunctory job of hand-washing before dinner, the helmet sent a tingle to his fingers to keep scrubbing. If the boy felt disposed to gluttony, the smart suit might tighten a gorget around his throat, making swallowing more difficult—or perhaps send a nauseating jolt to his belly-plate.

If an after-dinner stroll was advisable, the smart suit had Jonathan up and moving. If his stroll took him to an unexpectedly dangerous area, the GPS turned him around; and if he ever made a misstep, misstatement, or all-around poor decision, a superego-like voice in the helmet instantaneously set him to rights.

How proud the mad scientist and host mother had now grown of their once-helpless boy! He was smoothly navigating all of life's difficult patches without making any grievous errors. That of course was the idea: the smart suit would perfectly mold the boy's behavior, until at some indefinite future time it could be cast aside.

There was disagreement with the boy himself on this latter point, often quite sharp, as Jonathan grew up and came to regard the suit more and more as an impediment to social interaction. And his parents couldn't keep up the argument forever; as he approached his teens, their son became far too quick-witted to let any objections stand.

"Father and host mother, I assure you that I have assimilated all I can from the smart suit. Frankly, I would like to try on something more fashionable before I depart for university. Your fear that I may be going out into the world unprotected is unwarranted; on the contrary, let me assure you this constricting wrap is only holding me back!"

Then the young man, with his perfect complexion and smile of always well-tended teeth, announced he was going to take a bath to scrub off the funk of a dozen years.

He would be down later to show them. He *would* show them.

Jonathan trod up the stairs, leaving childhood behind him for good. His father and Imelda heard the door shut and lock; the sound of the bathwater running; and finally, a loud tearing *Zip!*

Then nothing further for the next hour except occasional

splashing in the tub. Happy-sounding plashes, for the most part.

Finally, Imelda could take no more waiting and ascended the stairs.

She knocked on the bathroom door.

A kind of gurgle came from within, but no answer.

A more concerned knock.

Again no answer. This time, she summoned Jonathan's father to help her force open the locked door.

They put their shoulders into it and heaved.

There they found Jonathan—babbling and befouling the tub, regressed all the way back to infancy.

"Are you OK?!" they asked.

But Jonathan's eyes didn't focus properly, and the only thing that formed on his lips was a spit bubble. No sign remained of the articulate, brilliant child prodigy in the smart suit.

"Ay, didn't I tell you?" sighed Imelda to his father. "Every year, all this new technology is just making everyone on the whole planet stupider and stupider."

The Princess Who Learned All-Is-One

Once a princess who was a fussy eater declared that henceforward, she would eat only one food at a time. She had done the same thing with her toys, favoriting a golden ball or musical instrument for a week, then clapping her hands for an attendant to toss it away on a dung-heap behind the castle.

That first week, it was nothing but carrots—fresh carrots, stewed carrots, carrots diced and whole. Since the girl was the imaginative sort, she became a rabbit and wrinkled her nose if Cook tried to hide any beans underneath her food, petulantly hopping away from the dining hall.

By the end of the week, the rabbit was hobbling. A glance in the princess's mirror revealed a shocking change in her complexion: her skin was as orange as an Oompa-Loompa's.

The second week, the princess chose to be a dog. She insisted that Cook pour her breakfast cereal out like dry kibble, and would only bark and lick her attendant's arm if the bowl was set on the floor.

For a couple of days, her health improved, although the excess sugar made her jittery. But soon the princess became whiney and whimpery, spending most of her time curled on the drawing room rug.

Her ankles and wrists swelled and she found it increasingly difficult to come up out of a crouch. When she did rise to her feet, she was bow-legged and stiff, like a rusty-armored knight.

Clearly, this diet was not working either. And so the princess thought and thought again, this time coming to the conclusion that cats must have the right idea about eating lots of meat. She ordered Cook to prepare strips of meat or fish and performed a little pantomime where she would bat at these with her fingertips, or snatch them out of her attendant's hands and scurry off with a sardine between her teeth.

Yet this game, too, ultimately had to be abandoned. The princess was napping constantly, her hair grew corkscrew, her gums turned red, and her teeth felt loose and too big for her mouth. She looked rather clowny, but didn't laugh at all because she had a nasty bout of diarrhea. Whenever she filled her chamberpot and summoned an attendant to come take it away, she was deeply embarrassed by the smell.

Out of worry for her daughter, the Queen felt obliged to put aside her royal scruples. She summoned an old woman who lived in the Dark Forest and was reputed to know many magic spells.

This old woman was ushered into the castle under armed guard in case she might be tempted to try any hoodoo. Then taken to the princess's bedchamber, where she found the little thing lying forlorn, eyes dull, unable to eat, as if life had become such a torment it was barely worth the bother.

The woman sniffed the air, grunted in disgust, put a hand on the princess's sweaty forehead, and produced a pill she ordered the sick girl to take with a glass of water. By this time, the tips of the guards' halberds were practically poking into the old woman's back, and they were really itching to run her through for having the effrontery to give their ruler's daughter orders. But the woman turned and gave them such a glare they stood down, for fear she was a gorgon.

The old woman ordered the princess to her feet, to look lively and march.

They made a slow progress out of the castle past all the shocked members of the court, and into the sunlight, which the princess had not seen in days. The guards trailed at a distance for the first part of the trek, but stopped at the edge of the Dark Forest, where devils were thought to dwell behind trees.

The woman led the princess through the woods, stopping here and there to pluck a wild onion, herb, or mushroom. She mumbled some sort of incantation about purifying the blood. They came to a tree bursting with nuts, and the woman ordered the princess to climb up and shake a branch. The old woman mentioned something about building strength.

The two stopped again at bushes where berries grew, and the old woman spoke cryptic words about growing new skin. She actually *ate* some berries on the spot and shared others with the princess. The girl was pleasantly shocked by the fresh burst of flavor. As the woman resumed her muttering, the princess realized it was not wholly nonsense, but part of an ancient prayer to the Earth Mother. This was disturbing, however—the Earth Mother was no longer an officially sanctioned god.

The old woman stopped at the garden plot outside her cottage, where she and the little princess spent a good half hour filling the basket with vegetables of all colors. Then the princess dutifully followed the woman into the dwelling and watched her boil water in a black cauldron big enough to roast a child.

The old woman followed the precepts of a secret formula, tossing in all the items they'd gathered, one-by-one. The princess helped stir.

Then the woman announced to the princess it was time. Sadly, the girl pulled a chair up to the cauldron and prepared to step in.

At this point in the story, the peasant woman clearly exceeded her social prerogatives, striking the noble girl with the back of her hand to prevent her from burning herself. She also called the princess a name I shall omit, as the tongue they spoke is a foreign one.

Finally, via a complex sequence of hand gestures, the woman managed to communicate to the misguided girl that she should eat her food, not swim in it.

And so they ate.

It was a meal of just one course, but it was enough.

Two Boys Who Amounted to Nothing

This story is not for the faint of heart. It involves two young men you may have heard of, who once gained modest notoriety in a coastal city for playing a kind of music that was lights out—or rather, which started slow and then got loud suddenly, like a raucous wake-up call.

Because the flannels they wore doubled as either pajama tops or shirts, and they could just pull jeans over the same underpants they'd slept in, getting up in the morning was never a rough transition for our lads, although rising before noon was indeed a foreign concept. Nor were they fond of cutting their hair, laundering their clothes, or eating anything green if there was a selection of fast-food restaurants nearby.

No doubt, the young men believed their lifestyle to be more radical and unconventional than it truly was, yet they took pride in their unwashed appearances, even throwing down a notorious challenge to one another. The rules for this "grunge match" were made up along the way, but it started simply enough, with seeing who could go the longest without a change of clothes. So of course, no showering either.

From this point, the duel escalated, going from no using Kleenex when a sleeve was available, to no washing hands before eating, to—perhaps I should have buried this in a footnote for the delicate reader—no washing up or wiping of any kind.

Fans of the music found themselves emulating the lads'

hygienic habits (or lack thereof); hence their private duel started a wave. Since the essence of this challenge involved "doing nothing" to groom oneself, it was inevitable that the band became known as the Nothings, and their fans the Do-Nothings.

Celebrity followed, and with it, money and TV appearances. The young men realized the time to call a truce to the grunge match was near at hand if they were going to be ready for their close-ups.

But this led to a bona fide life crisis. To their way of thinking, using shampoo or applying dehumanizing, scented deodorants could cause their righteousness to waft right off, and our lads became miserable at the very prospect of wearing anything that had to be hung or dry-cleaned. This felt to them like donning a commercial exoskeleton. Clothing was always better with wrinkles, because wrinkles allow one to move.

As for fine wining and dining—also overrated. True, those glory days of simply eating whatever was at hand when they were hungry hadn't been healthy, not at all, but neither was it good to ingest the rich, gout-worthy food they were now being offered at all hours of the night.

As for the Do-Nothings, they'd come to know the band through its first appearances and CDs, had mimicked the personal habits, and saw no reason not to continue on as before. They were certainly not going to dress up for a concert like it was a cotillion, nor remain seated if they could bounce up and down in a mosh pit. The two young men thought the fans had figured things out for themselves, possibly even eclipsed them when it came to authentic letting-go.

But the Do-Nothings wanted the two young men to continue to produce so they could consume. Hadn't the music, after all, always been about mindless consumption? Irony . . . what's that, yo?

The temptation to vanish off the grid became overwhelming for the band, even if it meant cancelling the rest of the appearances that year and turning down bucketloads of concert venue cash.

Rumors ensued of disappearances, drug overdoses, and death.

Time passed, and the group eventually sunk on the charts, allowing other, bottom-feeding bands to surface.

The Do-Nothings still maintained a Velcro-like solidarity as they traveled to other concerts, trying to carry on the spirit of raw lawlessness. But they were getting older. And meanwhile, where were the Nothings?

The Nothings, it turns out, had wisely invested part of their money in a small island on the outskirts of the city that first made them famous. Supplies were dropped off at monthly intervals, and album royalties were paid into a fractal-like network of foreign bank accounts to lead inquisitive journalists off the scent.

It was many years, in fact, before the two young men resumed any contact with others. In the interim, they grew up and became virtually unrecognizable. For they'd realized if time spent grooming one's hair was time wasted, you could either let it go, or just cut it all off. Why not?

And so the two shaved their heads.

If you didn't care to wear a shirt that constituted an advertisement for the soulless, sweatshop-sucking company that made it—and if, moreover, you believed clothes should be loose and comfortable and permit freedom of movement—why not wear a robe?

And so the two donned robes.

If a healthy meal that doesn't require much preparation is good enough for you, say maybe a slice of onion with tomato on a lox bagel, why not just eat when it's time to eat?

And so the two men remained off the clock when it came to mealtimes. Although they *did* tend to eat at the same time every day, as if a Pavlovian gong had sounded in their heads.

And I'm pleased to report that, over the years, their followers gradually did come back. The Do-Nothings were now middle-agers for whom "doing nothing" had become a truly paradoxical attainment, a utopian dream of relief from harried lives.

The two men allowed the occasional chartered boat to dock at their island, and sometimes sat down with little groups and led discussions.

I can't say whether they were ever recognized, or not.

Really, I don't think it would have made much difference.

Don't Bother Me, I'm Working

Our college custodian was about to reach the forty-year mark for service, and we all expected him to retire soon. Not due to any slow-down on the job; on the contrary, with his work ethic, he was a throwback to an earlier era. He never missed a day of work, and even as the campus had expanded over the decades, always shook off suggestions that he should have a team backing him.

All day long he'd be on call, roaming the grounds and look-ing around hopefully for litter, emptying trash bins whether they needed it or not. Bathrooms were touched up during the day, and class cancellations afforded an opportunity to scrub dry-erase boards or windows. By mid-afternoon, the hum of his vacuum could be heard in the cafeteria; and over weekends, he could be found on site deep cleaning or buffing floors.

Conversations with him tended to be over before they started, his replies limited to "Got to go," or a gruff, "Don't bother me, I'm working."

But things came to a head when the administration decided to commemorate the man's four decades of service with a fab-ulous vacation. A plaque or gold watch didn't seem sufficient reward for someone who'd never even taken a sick day; and besides, the school needed to lock up over the July recess to cut down on operating costs.

The presentation line-up in the banquet room that day included the Dean and several faculty. A cake was cut and paper plates passed around, but our man looked like he'd rather be standing there with a trash bag.

What really made him uncomfortable was being handed an envelope and asked to say a few words. He stammered out a thank-you and put the envelope in his pocket, but the Dean told him to open it.

There would be no quick escape.

The man's expression fell as he pulled out a plane ticket and copy of a hotel reservation at a swank Central American resort. He actually tried to pass off the envelope to someone else, a new faculty member who looked up to the Dean hopefully, but the Dean gave her a stern look.

As the one designated to give the custodian his lift to the airport, I can attest that he was ill-suited to be a tourist. His only luggage was a professor's cast-off briefcase. Presumably, it was roomy enough to contain shorts and beachwear, because he still wore his janitor's uniform.

He looked rather like a death row inmate headed to execution. And as I led him to the van I almost did joke, "Dead man walking."

Of course I didn't. In fact, we hardly spoke.

A few days later, I received an "urgent" email with a link to a news report. A Costa Rican reporter stood on a street front, a luxury resort in the background. Windows had been smashed, refuse was everywhere, and I didn't need subtitles to catch the word *terrorista*. The message had come from the executive office along with a summons to an emergency meeting. I put two-and-two together and realized the hotel was the same one where we'd just sent our most valued employee.

The news on the ground was as bad as we'd feared. Not all the guests had been accounted for, and our custodian topped the list of those missing.

That night I found myself on a red-eye flight with the Dean. He was there to sort out the liability issues; I was there for the grislier purpose of potentially identifying the body.

Our ride from the airport was even grimmer. The closer we drew to the hotel, the thicker the trail of devastation. But the word on the street differed from what we'd heard on TV. Our cab driver spoke, not of a terrorist strike, but of a lone "wild man" who'd emerged from the jungle and gone on a rampage through the posh tourist district. And this was more than just rumor: the wild man had been caught!

The cabby flashed us a picture from the morning paper of the shaggy haired perp, unshaven, with crazy eyes. Some bruises suggesting he may have been roughed up by local police. But something else, too.

I leaned forward. "Take us to the jail instead," I said.

It took hours to push past the red tape, and the Dean had to grease more than a few wheels, but we eventually got to see the prisoner.

He was peacefully sweeping out his cell, still in his janitor's uniform.

What had driven him temporarily insane, he later told us, were the pristine beaches and luxury accommodations. Work was this man's religion, and there'd been nothing for him to clean, nothing to do.

So he'd created his own mess.

"I was going to clean it up," he apologized.

The Dean did not un-grit his teeth. But somehow he managed to obtain permission for the man to undo the damage he'd caused—legs chained together, two guards' rifles pointed on him the entire time.

And despite these hindrances, he did an immaculate job.

The hotel didn't wish to create an international incident and was more than willing to downgrade *terrorista* to crazed *turista*. That is how, one week later, vacation over, we found ourselves on a plane back.

"Do you have any idea what this little incident is going to cost the school?" the Dean asked.

"No," our man truthfully replied.

"You'd have to work it off till the day you die."

The custodian smiled.

I've never seen a man look happier.

Ordering Off the Menu

Oh, the Blogger Troll! Feared by restaurateurs everywhere! With his giant nose for snuffling, warty tongue, and huge underteeth that jutted above his lower lip, giving him a disdainful smirk! He was notorious for visiting dining establishments by day and hunching over his computer all night, writing the most terrible reviews.

But a young woman named Arnette knew that a kind word from the Blogger Troll could also make a restaurant a success. She'd studied to be a chef for years before opening her own place, and only when she felt ready, invited the great critic to sample the menu.

On the appointed evening, the Blogger Troll, escorted by a handful of servants, arrived and took his seat at a table, and was brought the menu. He studied it briefly, unmoved by the dazzling selections of entrées and side dishes. Then banged his fist on the table to order.

The server timidly approached and asked, "Are you ready? What shall I fetch you?"

The Blogger Troll started enumerating dishes in unexpected and riotous combinations. It was all the server could do to keep up.

Back in the kitchen, Arnette threw her hands in the air.

"I should've known he would do this!" she said. "Dishes that needed to be broiled, boiled, barbecued, baked, seared, sautéed, and lightly toasted all at once!" She made a good effort to get everything ready, but some items naturally took longer than others, and emerged before they were optimally done.

When the food was brought to the Blogger Troll, he placed a finger over one of his nostrils and bent over the table. He took a mighty sniff, then shook his head. He alternated nostrils and took another sniff. He started to lower his tongue, lower, lower, lower until the tip touched the sauce on his dish. His taste buds looked as big as tire treads!

As he tasted the food, The Blogger Troll's googly eyes rolled back in his head.

Suddenly, he spit the sauce out in a great gob on his plate.

He announced, "You are not ready yet. I shall return to this spot in exactly four years."

Then he got up, pushed in his chair, and left with his followers, who shook their fists in the air and made angry noises.

Over the next four years, Arnette expanded her kitchen and practiced every method of preparing food until no living chef was more adept than her. She also digitized her menu to make it interactive, allowing for thousands of new combinations. For the night the Blogger Troll was expected to return, she brought on extra kitchen staff to help her. She felt she was ready.

Right on time, snorting noises and heavy footsteps could be heard coming up the steps. As you may know, trolls' knees do not bend, hence they are noisy walkers.

The Blogger Troll entered, looking as grim as ever, and took his seat. He was handed the new interactive menu, which surprised him.

For a while, he became distracted scrolling up and down pages without clicking on anything. Then he turned off the tablet and handed it back to the server.

"I'll be ordering off the menu tonight," he said. And he began to name a long list of exotic dishes along with his special instructions.

When Arnette saw the list, she did a double take. But by this time, she'd become perhaps the greatest chef in the world, and rose to the challenge. She called together her staff and gave orders. Some of the Troll's instructions involved herbs and rare fungi that could only be found growing under remote bridges. Arnette had to make clever substitutions using the ingredients she had.

And what she presented to the Blogger Troll was, unquestionably, a great feast.

This time, after sniffing his plate with one nostril, then another, and dipping his grotesque tongue down to his plate, the Troll actually took a bite and chewed, making his pointy ears wiggle.

He opened his mouth for a second bite, and as he did, morsels fell out between the gaps in his lower teeth. (*Ew!*)

He chewed again, frowned in concentration, but then again shook his head.

"You are not ready yet," he announced. "I shall return to this spot in exactly two years."

He rose from the table abruptly, knocking his chair over, and left.

"At least he tried his food this time," Arnette sighed. And then she went back to work.

Over the next two years, she mastered each recipe until she'd gotten every texture and savor just right. And then she put the cookbooks away and just created on her own.

At the appointed hour, the Blogger Troll entered the restaurant. It had been stripped of decorations because the expanded kitchen left room for only a couple of tables. The Troll made a note of these changes as if to later fault the restaurant for its lack of ambiance.

But even if Arnette had noticed his reaction, she probably wouldn't have cared much. By this point, it was the food and only the food that mattered to her.

The Troll thumped his great fist on the table. "Bring me the menu!" he ordered.

The server approached. "I'm sorry, sir, but there is no menu in this restaurant."

"No menu? Then what is there to order?"

"Anything you like."

The Blogger Troll looked confused for a moment, and then he laughed.

"Just bring me a steak," he said. "Blood rare."

The steak was brought out along with a sampling of Arnette's recent creations.

And on his blog that night, the Troll wrote: "The Best Food Anywhere."

The Giant Who Practiced Kinhin

A giant six stories tall once resided near the valley of Attan, land that is now mostly desert. He spent most of his time in the mountains, which felt more suitably proportioned to him, and where it was always a simple matter to pluck a goat off the slopes, pop it into his mouth, and afterwards pick his teeth with the horns.

One day as he tromped along through a mountain pass, he caught some slight movement near the top of a peak. He was hugely farsighted, like all giants, so after he grabbed the creature from the mountainside he held it at arm's length to view it.

What gradually came into focus in the curl of his palm was a wizened old man.

This little man was taking very deliberate steps along the calloused lines of the giant's hand, pivoting when he came to the thenar of the thumb, and then carefully reversing direction until he hit the rise on the ulnar side, just below the pinkie.

For some reason, the giant did not consider eating this little man with the toy soldier gait. I wouldn't say he refrained out of "natural curiosity"; curiosity is no more a quality of giants than it is of brickbats. Let's settle instead for "dumb stupefaction."

After ten minutes of watching the odd fellow pace back and forth, the giant impatiently cleared his throat with a rumble that shook the mountain ridge and caused a rain of boulders.

"Old man, are you blind to where you are stepping, or simply out of your mind?"

The odd little man stopped. He gazed up at the giant with a blissful look on his face.

"I am practicing *kinhin*, or walking meditation," he replied.

"And you do not fear me?" spoke the giant, astonished.

The wizened one smiled and continued to pace. He was so eager to resume his serene routine that he didn't notice when the giant returned him to the ridge where he'd found him. Nearby was the thatch hut where he lived in solitary pursuit of truth.

The giant had done the simple calculation that he must be a wizard, and he knew enough to leave wizards alone. So he was about to go, but just at that moment, the old man completed the exact number of steps he'd set out to take that morning, which was one thousand-and-eight.

He stopped and addressed the giant. "Would you like to learn?"

And in this manner the giant became the old man's pupil.

The giant spent several weeks near the old man's hut, observing his methods and practicing pacing through the mountain pass, until he, too, had learned to match his thoughts to his steps. He learned "going without arriving": the idea of just walking to walk, not to forage for food or meet up with other giants, who never got along with each other anyway.

He learned to "shake off the burden of worries": to relax and step with complete freedom.

He learned the "emperor's seal," the firm and deliberate placement of feet on the ground. He was quite good at this, because *all* giants enjoyed stamping their feet emphatically and making the ground thunder. He felt truly at peace with himself, in touch with his giant-ness.

Yet he grew restless to move on. "Really, this *kinhin* is something giants were born for," he boasted to himself. "To walk straight onward, taking stout steps—I did not need the old man to teach me this. And I must be moving on, since there is nothing left to eat in this valley."

Sensing the imminent defection of his pupil, the guru tried to reason with him.

"But you have not yet learned, 'a lotus flower blooms beneath each step,'" he told the giant. "You have not yet learned the Ultimate Purpose."

The giant shook off these words and departed abruptly, with long strides, putting as much distance as he could between himself and his teacher.

After several days, he'd traversed most of the mountain ridge and come to a valley which looked most promising for *kinhin*. In truth, he had missed the feeling of peace and serenity. And so he decided to make up for lost time by practicing all afternoon.

"I shall take one million-and-eight steps!" he vowed.

You probably know the rest of the story. The destruction of the great civilization of Attan is a tragedy of ancient history, yet an enduring mystery, long believed to have been the work of an asteroid or earthquake.

Really, it was all due to the giant and his *kinhin*: marching up and down the fertile valley with complete abandon, unknowingly putting the "seal of the emperor" on houses and buildings and delicate temples. Only when he'd completed one million-and-eight steps did the giant look back.

Attan had been completely destroyed, reduced to a flat plain.

The realization that he may have horribly misstepped began

to seep into the giant's thick skull. And thus in great haste he returned to the wizened guru in the thatched hut.

Sheepishly, he bowed his head.

"I am ready to resume my teaching, Master."

The old man acknowledged him with only a brief nod.

"Please tell me, what is 'the lotus flower blooms'?"

"To appreciate the miracle of life wherever one steps."

"And the Ultimate Purpose?"

"The Ultimate Purpose is to spread compassion."

Then and there, the giant froze in his tracks. Somewhere in his depths, a caring for others had suddenly blossomed. He realized he could never take another step for fear of hurting another creature.

He stands there still, forming part of the mountain range.

Passing locals used to place fingers to lips and whisper "Shhh!" so as not to awaken him. Over the centuries, the sibilant became attached to the mountain's name, which is today pronounced "Mt. Kin-Shen."

A Black Hole the Size of a Pea

Once a king on a faraway planet had a daughter, Jupar, of whom he was very, very protective. Girls were a rare commodity on this world; the race had evolved from bee colonies, it was said. The people there were squat and bulbous and a little orange-furry.

Every three years during the mating season, it was as though a switch had been thrown in the kingdom, and all of the male drones would be overtaken by hormones and caught up in a frenzy. And really there was nothing to do for it except barricade the castle and lock Jupar in a tower. She was the only survivor of several generations of sisters.

The king's motives in keeping his virgin daughter protected in this manner were two-fold. One, he didn't think Jupar quite old enough to go out alone into the congregating area, where she'd be swarmed. Second, in order to keep the bloodline pure as possible, he wanted to have some say over the twelve-to-seventeen courtiers expected to mate with her.

Therefore at all times, Jupar remained surrounded by ladies-in-waiting who were themselves workers, infertile. These ladies tried to keep tabs on the princess, who was starting to feel the urgent call to slip out of the castle to relieve herself of her eggs.

Fortunately for the king, space travel had advanced in this civilization far beyond my capacity to explain it to you, and he was able to concoct a most ingenious plan. He sent his most trustworthy guards on a mission to obtain a small black hole, the tiniest possible.

At first, the thinking may have been to use the black hole as a kind of drone-zapper, to clear the congregating area of hormone-crazed males who would be sucked into the vortex with no messy clean-up. But that is not really how event horizons work. Read a little more, and you will see.

The guards returned from outer space with a container that resembled a mini nuclear reactor, no bigger than a lantern. This container was taken out to the middle of the castle courtyard at night when no one could observe. And opened by a volunteer, a brave man with no family, whose name now most certainly belongs on a wall of heroes.

The next day, space and time began to bend around the black hole, with interesting results: passing birds, carriages, and parasols had become constellated around it in a kind of topiary, which shone a lovely crimson. Objects weren't sucked immediately into the void, nor were the princess's suitors, who'd come buzzing along right on schedule.

They were spaghettified, true, but this actually made them less squat-looking, in my opinion. Frozen on their faces was a look of lust mixed with surprise. But no one was in danger of dying, which is saying a lot for an ephemeral species derived from flying insects. Rather, while caught up in that place where time stopped, people could live forever, or at least for eternity-minus.

Suddenly, Jupar broke through her gauntlet of ladies-in-waiting and ran into the courtyard. She tried to stop when she saw the giant orb, but the animal magnetism which had drawn her toward the suitors in the first place was enough to overcome all resistance.

Soon she, too, was stuck there.

Next from the castle came the ladies-in-waiting, who, in trying to pull the princess down with their butterfly nets, were predictably trapped themselves.

The king, left alone, regarded this scene from his window. He observed the tiny black hole, now with well-dressed ladies and gentlemen caught in its field. The populace was in no apparent distress, greeting one another amicably, as if at a ball rather than trapped up in one.

And there was his daughter, looking slimmer and less strained by her eggs, glad to be part of the scene for once rather than cooped up in the castle.

The king shut his window. He had done this terrible thing of stopping time—no denying that guilty fact. And there was no way to turn off a black hole.

It was several days before the king summoned the wherewithal to look out his window again. Yes—the orb was still there, hovering several feet off the ground, and all the rest of his subjects had since joined in, or been sucked in during rescue ops, for there were brooms and ladders and long poles floating in the crimson. It was with some difficulty that he was able to spot his daughter at all, but there she was, ruddy-complected and happy, carrying on a conversation with a young gentleman; somehow they'd managed to join hands, and it didn't look like they'd ever let go.

He shut the window again, but this time thought, *And what of me? A king with no subjects?*

He felt that he'd aged a great deal with worry in the past week, while the same could never be said for his subjects or his daughter. All were spinning along just fine without him.

Unintentionally, he'd realized a selfish parent's wish: a

beloved child who could never grow old, never have to survive the violence of mating season, never have to die. Jupar was one of the immortals.

Slowly, the king rose from his throne and climbed painfully up the spiral staircase to the top of the tower. He stepped onto the parapet and leaned out as far as he could.

Just a few feet below, the giant red ball floated, rotating slowly, hypnotically.

Then the king clapped his hands to command everyone's attention.

"Geronimo!" he yelled, jumping towards eternity.

Master of All

Once upon a space-time continuum, two interplanetary travelers of very different species crossed paths at the edge of a vast solar system.

There were twenty-seven more-or-less habitable planets in it, and almost a thousand mineral-rich moons. Each explorer was attempting to lay claim to as much territory as possible in the name of his race. One was known as Zav, and the other one called Oon.

It so happened that Zav arrived on site a moment earlier than Oon, and this fact ended up making all the difference. He had done some prior charting of the system and discovered that along the perimeter was a wicked anomaly, a space-time curvature that made the system impossible to circumnavigate.

Knowing this, he decided to see if Oon might be convinced to go along with a little ruse.

"Let us not quibble," crackled Zav's voice over the communicator. "We might as well make a sport of it. Whoever flies around this system first can keep it—lock, stock, and barium."

"I don't know. What have you been up to all this time?" Oon asked, suspiciously.

"Ship repairs," Zav lied.

Oon didn't trust this reply, but nonetheless believed he had the faster vessel.

"You're on," he agreed.

And before another word could be said, Oon gunned his rockets.

"Oho!" said Zav, rubbing his hands together. "Very soon, I shall be Master of All."

He watched on his monitor as Oon's craft began its orbit. Without warning, it hit the space-time curve hard and started to veer sideways. And as the curve steepened, the ship suddenly jumped out of its trajectory, disappearing in a burst of light.

"He will be rerouted to the far side of the galaxy," Zav reflected. And he went on his own victory lap around the twenty-seven planets, careful to avoid all the bumps.

"I am Master of All!" he gloated.

The thought of owning an entire solar system was so appealing that Zav decided to give up his exploring career. Why leave, when he had what he had, unchecked domain over many worlds, sweetened with the memory of outfoxing his opponent? Not only this, but several of the planets turned out to be inhabited by friendly creatures who were pleasant enough to be around, even if they were his inferiors.

So for many years, Zav presided happily over his interplanetary empire, amusing himself by designing elaborate monuments for his slave armies to build. They regarded their heavenly visitor as a god, of course.

Only when he was several centuries old and becoming too infirm and tired to go on much longer did Zav have his first thought in many years of poor Oon.

"At least I am better off than that fellow," he reflected aloud. "At least I can go to my rest not as an eternal wanderer, but as Master of All."

But only a few weeks later, Zav had an unexpected visitor.

Someone who he had no trouble recognizing after so many years, someone who returned appearing not to have aged at all, someone who arrived in a corona of shining light.

"Zav, you old rascal," said the voice, which had a semi-divine echo built into it, as if emanating from Mt. Olympus. "I bet you never counted on seeing me again!"

"True," admitted Zav.

There was an awkward pause, and then Zav added: "I suppose I'd better apologize for sending you on that wild goose chase."

"No need to apologize," replied Oon. "For you see, I suspected time was going to curve."

"Oh?" said Zav.

"The only question was, to where?" said Oon. "And unlike you, I thought I might as well take my chances. 'No risk it, no biscuit.'"

"So where did you end up?" asked Zav, feigning indifference.

"Nowhere at all, for many centuries. Just imagine how I hated you! But then space-time began to curve again, and again, until I'd reached the very edge of the universe!"

"Of this universe, anyway," he corrected himself. "From the outlying areas, you can clearly see outward onto many better ones."

"Never knew it," said Zav.

"I have gazed into infinity," Oon said, with faraway eyes. "I have seen into the Eleventh Dimension. I have observed parallel universes and universes in bubbles. I have watched the great Dark Flow, and visited the secret spawning grounds of black holes. And then, after many years, I decided to continue on my way, until I arrived back at this very spot where we started our little game."

"I see," said Zav, who wasn't sure he did.

"Yes, it's true," said Oon. "We agreed that whoever circled this system first would win it—although I must say, after seeing more of what's out there, this place is no great shakes. But a bet is a bet."

"I was just on my way out," said Zav.

"Oh?" Oon refocused his far-flung vision onto Zav for the first time and perceived that his former nemesis was dying.

"I had a good run," Zav said.

"I suppose you may die here, if you must. I wasn't planning on staying. Really, the secret to staying young is to keep moving as long as possible. To be Master of All is to be Master of Nothing, in the banal sense of hanging around and giving orders. Rather, it is to remain free in time, in complete harmony with the flow of things."

Hearing those words, Zav died.

Without dwelling too long on the matter, Oon picked up the desiccated husk of his former foe and carried it off under one arm.

I'll incinerate this in the sun on my way out, he thought.

The Old Man Who Lived in the Now

A man spent most of his adult life postponing the idea of going abroad, expressing the opinions that it was (1) too dangerous; and (2) a waste of money.

His wife finally countered these objections by entering a contest for an all-expenses paid vacation, winning it, and then displaying the tickets, arguing that if the valuable prize went unused, who is the waster now?

Unfortunately, two weeks later when the man and his wife were sitting at a sidewalk café in a quaint foreign piazza, a boy riding a bakery delivery bicycle sped around a sharp corner and a hardened baguette launched itself from his satchel like a lance. It delivered a direct blow to the man's forehead, right to his third eye chakra.

The old man was not badly hurt, but got up shakily from his place at the table.

His wife snapped, "Where are you going?"

The man replied, "Who are you?"

For he was living in the Now. The past had ceased to exist for him.

He continued down the street until he came to a fair where vendors sold sandwiches, wraps, and delectable confections. The old man felt the call of hunger, grabbed a sandwich, and began to eat. As he took a bite he remarked, "This bite is good." Then he took another and remarked, "This bite is good." And so it went for the whole meal.

The old man felt thirst and asked for a drink. "How about paying for that sandwich first?" the proprietor retorted. But you see, the old man had been following the primal call of appetite and was unable to recall any "pay-for-this" protocols, nor form any concept of consequences such as "going to jail." The future didn't exist for him, either.

The vendor decided to let this one go, reasoning that the old man must be suffering from dementia. And so the old man continued to roam freely about the street fair. Until he felt an urgent urge to urinate, and unceremoniously dropped his pants in the middle of the crowd.

A novel series of Now moments followed. In one, he felt the bite of handcuffs while smelling odors of frying meats and fresh-baked pies. In one, he stood before a magistrate while a stern-sounding sentence was handed down in a foreign tongue. In one, he found himself sitting in a cool cell with a cot and seat-less toilet. In between Nows, the old man drifted in and out of consciousness.

Surprisingly, he thrived in his new surroundings. The next morning a tray was slid under the grate of his cell and he became conscious of hunger. After eating, he felt sleepy and lay on the cot. When he awoke, he felt the need to relieve himself and the toilet was right there. In hours to come, the whole cycle was to repeat itself with monastic regularity, though the man could not have anticipated this. He was just doing the immediate thing.

The second day in the jail was the repeat of the first, with the surprise addition of a morning bowel movement. The third day offered a repeat of the second. And this routine repeated itself for some days, only broken by the unexpected appearance of an elderly woman and two white-coated attendants outside the cell.

The mysterious old woman offered the man her hand, and he took it. She pointed the way out of the cell, and he followed, the two white-coated men finding it unnecessary to hold either arm. A series of Now moments ensued that included airports, car rides, and a hospital check-in.

The man's doctor, Dr. Gupta, was a specialist assigned to dementia patients, but soon his battery of tests began to yield surprising results. For when it was not his naptime, the old man was able to engage with his surroundings in a highly alert, perceptive way. An EEG revealed that brain activity was unusually active in the baguette area, and the old man responded to patient-care protocols intuitively and accurately.

He was fully present in the moment. True, he had lost the vestiges of ego, but from a spiritual perspective, this could be considered a tremendous advantage. The doctors and interns who lined up to study the celebrity patient arrived with one set of medical questions and ended up asking questions of a whole other sort: "What are you able to see in a 'moment'?" "How long does it last, and what sorts of things get connected together in it?" "Can others experience this 'moment' with you?"

The patient had become the teacher.

Keeping the old man institutionalized couldn't be justified for long when there is so much beauty in this world for us to appreciate.

The old man was taken out by generous interns, brought to seascapes and mountains, concerts and fashion shows.

His opinions were solicited by interns who became fast friends, or even ended up marrying one another. For they'd shared experiences together as only the old man could have laid them out, in all of their complexity and macro-connectedness and transient splendor.

Though in his last years the old man was confined to a wheelchair, he was still able to hold a baby or bunny, or pull himself up to table for a fine dining experience. True, each bite was always the only bite for him, each meal the best, eaten at the precise point of hunger, never too soon or too late. And if there was a savor to savor, a special hint of freshness or whole-someness to enjoy, such pleasures never escaped him.

He retained to the end his ability to penetrate the Now and share it, and so through him and by him, the world was made a richer place. Did you get a chance to know him? I did.

I was one of those interns. And I can feel the old man's presence now, even as I bring his story to a close.

About the Author

M.V. Montgomery is the author of numerous books of poetry and fiction, including the fantasy collections *What We Did with Old Moons*, *Beyond the Pale*, and *Speculations*, all from Winter Goose Publishing. He teaches at Life University.